D1621981

this
•little• barron's•
book belongs to

....

....

First edition for the United States and Canada published 2000 by
Barron's Educational Series, Inc.

Copyright © Nicola Smee 2000

First published in Great Britain by Orchard Books in 2000.

All inquiries should be addressed to:
Barron's Educational Series, Inc.
250 Wireless Boulevard, Hauppauge, New York 11788
http://www.barronseduc.com

Library of Congress Catalog Card No.: 99-68443
International Standard Book No. 0-7641-1580-4

Printed in Italy

9 8 7 6 5 4 3 2 1

Freddie Goes on an Airplane

Nicola
Smee

· little · barron's ·

We're going to Spain
on an AIRPLANE
to see my Uncle Teddy.

At the airport we show our tickets and passport but . . .

before we can board the airplane
our carry-on bags have to be x-rayed.

When our seatbelts are fastened, the airplane gets ready for take-off and the engines

ROAR!

Then up, up, up we go....

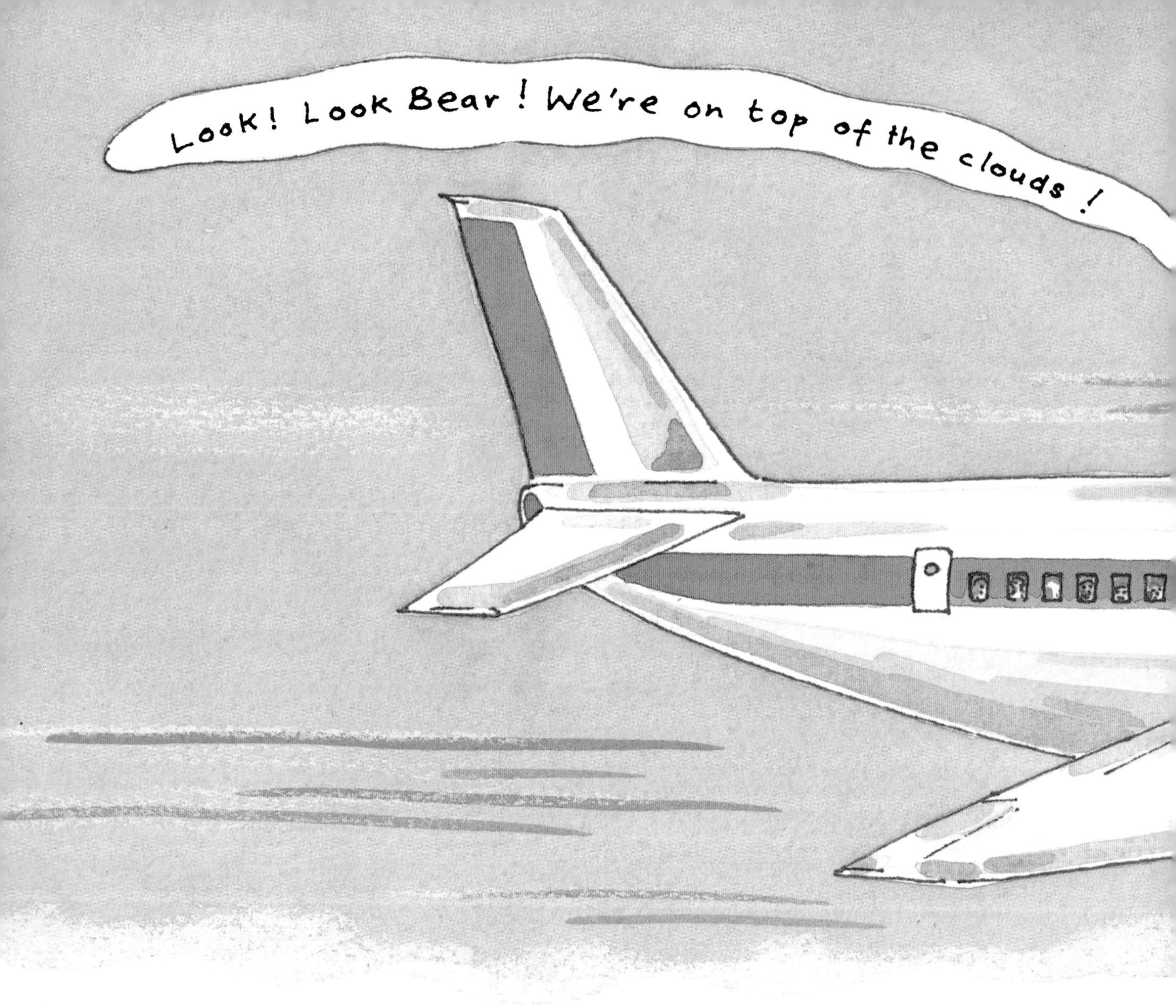
Look! Look Bear! We're on top of the clouds!

...up into the clear blue sky.

The attendant gives us some
crayons and paper.

And later, some food and drink.

When we start to land we have sweets
to suck on so our ears don't go 'pop'!

I show the attendant my pictures
and she says she hopes I fly
on her airplane again.

Then we have to wait for our luggage to come around on the carousel.